# BIG RIG BUGS

## KURT CYRUS

Walker & Company  New York

Love and hugs

to all the bugs

Splat.

Squish.

Tuna fish.

Pickles. Beans.

Turnip greens.

Big rigs roll
from every hole.

Take the lead,
millipede.

Clear that thicket,
dozer cricket.

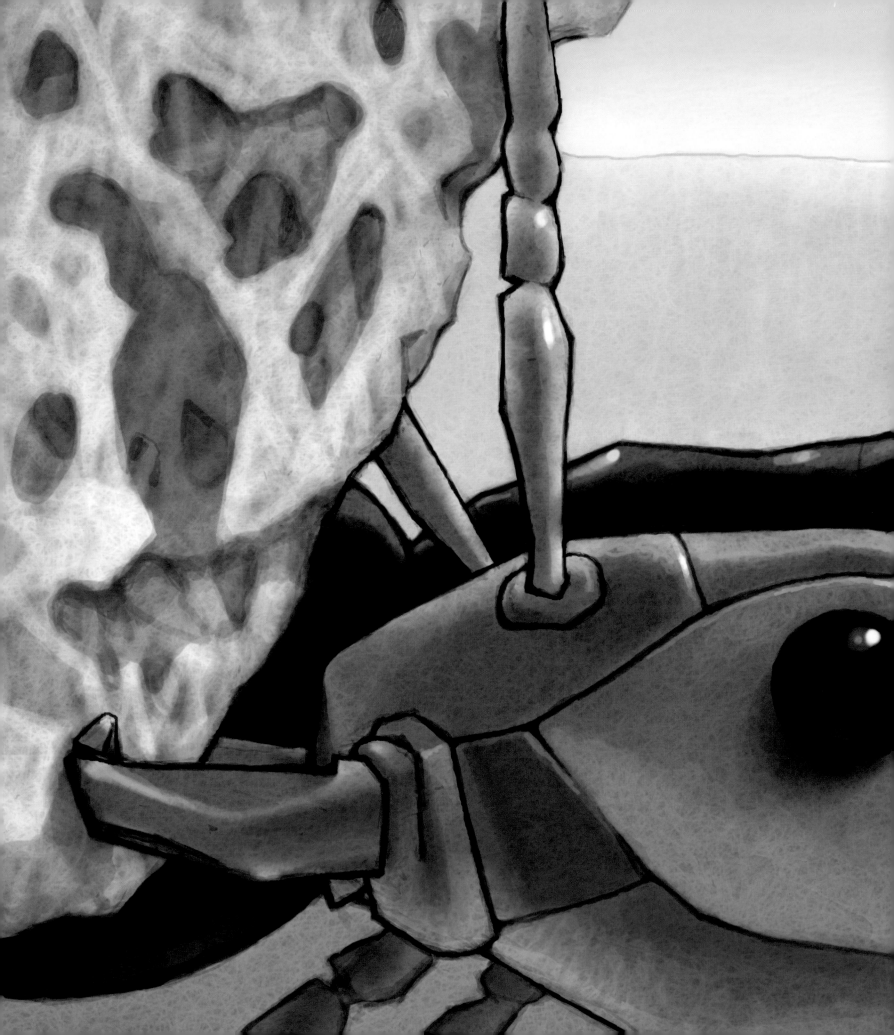

Ants that lift,
sort, and sift.

Weevil drill
takes a spill.

Earwig loader
revs its motor.

Move that muck,
beetle truck.

Pack it firm,
pickleworm.

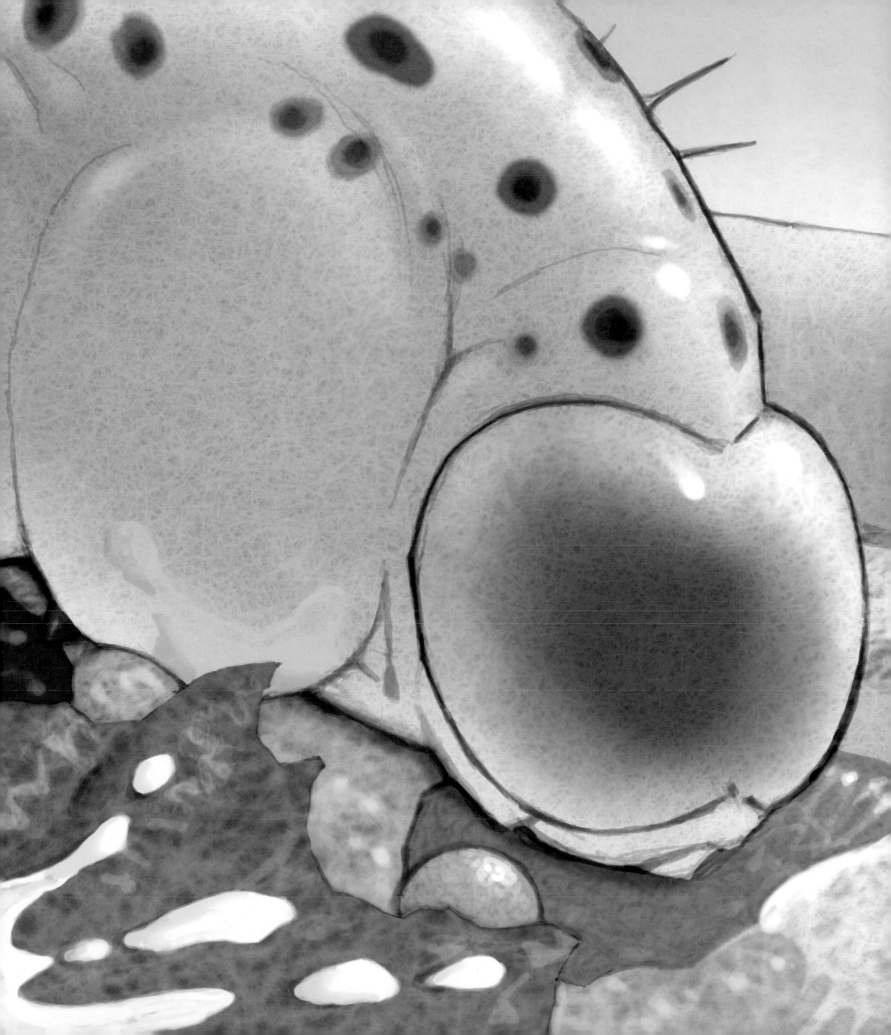

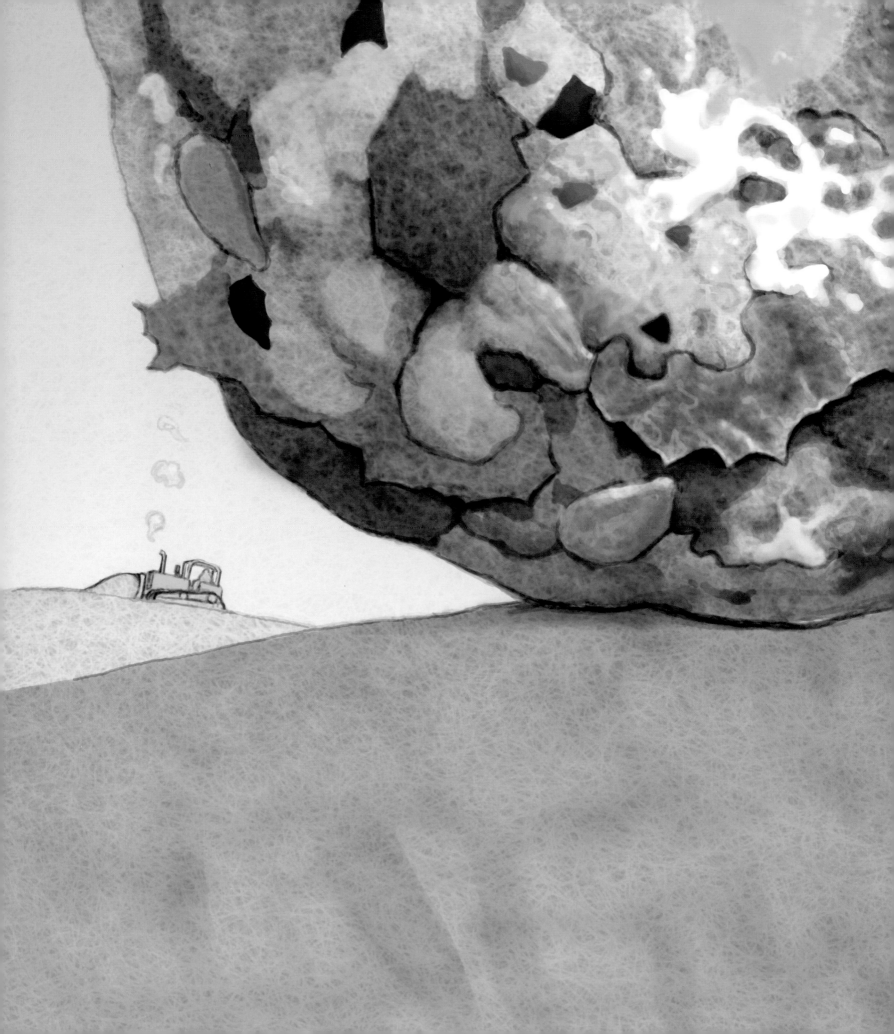

Chug, chug, chug,
tumblebug.

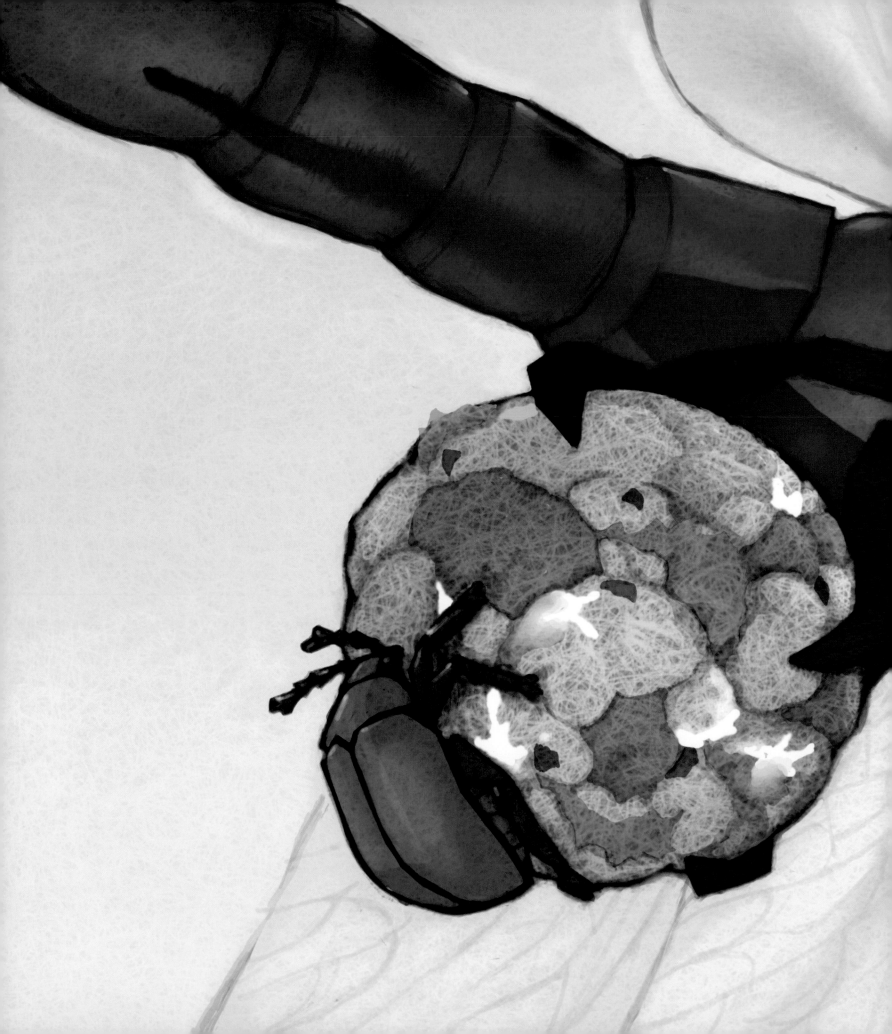

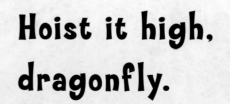

Hoist it high,
dragonfly.

Job well done,
everyone.

Backward creep—
*beeeep, beeeep.*

See you later,
excavator.

First published in the United States of America in May 2010 by
Walker Publishing Company, Inc., a division of Bloomsbury Publishing, Inc.
Visit Walker & Company's Web site at www.bloomsburykids.com

For information about permission to reproduce selections from this book, write to
Permissions, Walker & Company, 175 Fifth Avenue, New York, New York 10010

Library of Congress Cataloging-in-Publication Data
Cyrus, Kurt.
Big rig bugs / by Kurt Cyrus.—1st U.S. ed.
        p.        cm.
Summary: Insects resemble heavy equipment as they clean up some litter.
ISBN 978-0-8027-8674-6 (hardcover) · ISBN 978-0-8027-8688-3 (reinforced)
[1. Stories in rhyme. 2. Insects—Fiction. 3. Trucks—Fiction.] I. Title.
PZ8.3.C997Bi 2010           [E]—dc22           2009029917

Illustrations drawn and colored digitally
Typeset in Typography of Coop Heavy
Book design by Danielle Delaney

Printed in China by Hung Hing Printing (China) Co. Ltd., Shenzhen, Guangdong
2 4 6 8 10 9 7 5 3 (hardcover)
2 4 6 8 10 9 7 5 3 (reinforced)

All papers used by Walker & Company are natural, recyclable products
made from wood grown in well-managed forests. The manufacturing processes
conform to the environmental regulations of the country of origin.